To Mi'kma'ki, to the water —
to all family and friends who took me there, and to all who protect it.
—J.W.

Copyright © 2023 by Jack Wong

All rights reserved. Published by Orchard Books, an imprint of Scholastic Inc., *Publishers since 1920*. ORCHARD BOOKS and design are registered trademarks of Watts Publishing Group, Ltd., used under license. SCHOLASTIC and associated logos are trademarks and/or registered trademarks of Scholastic Inc. • The publisher does not have any control over and does not assume any responsibility for author or third-party websites or their content. • No part of this publication may be reproduced, stored in a retrieval system, or transmitted in any form or by any means, electronic, mechanical, photocopying, recording, or otherwise, without written permission of the publisher. For information regarding permission, write to Scholastic Inc., Attention: Permissions Department, 557 Broadway, New York, NY 10012. • This book is a work of fiction. Names, characters, places, and incidents are either the product of the author's imagination or are used fictitiously, and any resemblance to actual persons, living or dead, business establishments, events, or locales is entirely coincidental.

Library of Congress Cataloging-in-Publication Data Available

ISBN 978-1-338-83096-5

10 9 8 7 6 5 4 3 2 1   23 24 25 26 27

Printed in China   38

First edition, May 2023

Book design by Doan Buu and Patti Ann Harris

The text and display type were set in Baskervilla Com.

The illustrations were created with pastels and watercolor.

When You Can Swim

by Jack Wong

Orchard Books
an Imprint of Scholastic Inc.
New York

When you can swim,
first I'll take you to the ocean

past the sandpipers tracing
the shape of a wave on the shore
past the edge of wet
splashing at your ankles

to receive the water's welcome.

When you can swim,
you'll know how to float
just lying on your back
watching treetops drift by

and I'll lift my head to make sure
the shore hasn't wandered too far
just remember to wriggle
your toes now and then.

When you can swim,
you'll reach landscapes as foreign as the moon
no spaceship required

except the craters are
squishy and filled with reeds
ready to swallow loose sandals
but like good explorers we'll leave only footprints.

When you can swim,
we'll bend like boulders
beneath rushing waterfalls

letting the current carry midday sun
from upstream down to our shoulders
letting it make us round and whole.

When you can swim,
we'll listen to the clinking
of waves passing in and out
of a million pebbles
telling of countless days
and months and years
telling of caves that lie
beyond that rocky point
then we'll tumble
into the water
as the pebbles do.

When you can swim,
you'll rise before even the sun
wondering if the smoke on the lake
is really a steaming sauna that would make
a perfect remedy for brisk morning air

then jump in and see for yourself
just how balmy the water is.

When you can swim,
we'll slip into the pond at dusk
when the fish awaken in air
feasting on twilight's bugs

we'll tread still and quiet
not to disturb their work
just to watch the ripples
break the surface.

When you can swim,
I'll count you down if you dare to dive
off the bridge over the canal

underneath is an amphitheater
laced with late afternoon light
that will echo your voice
a thousand times over
if you also dare to sing.

When you can swim,
you'll conquer any fear
of tannin-soaked lakes
pitch-dark from tree bark
like oversteeped tea
because that darkness
will turn glittering gold
when you gather it
by the handful.

When you can swim,
we'll set our sights on that little island
where I know the blueberries
are sweetest every summer

it'll look close enough
but prove farther at halfway
then the whitecaps will pick up

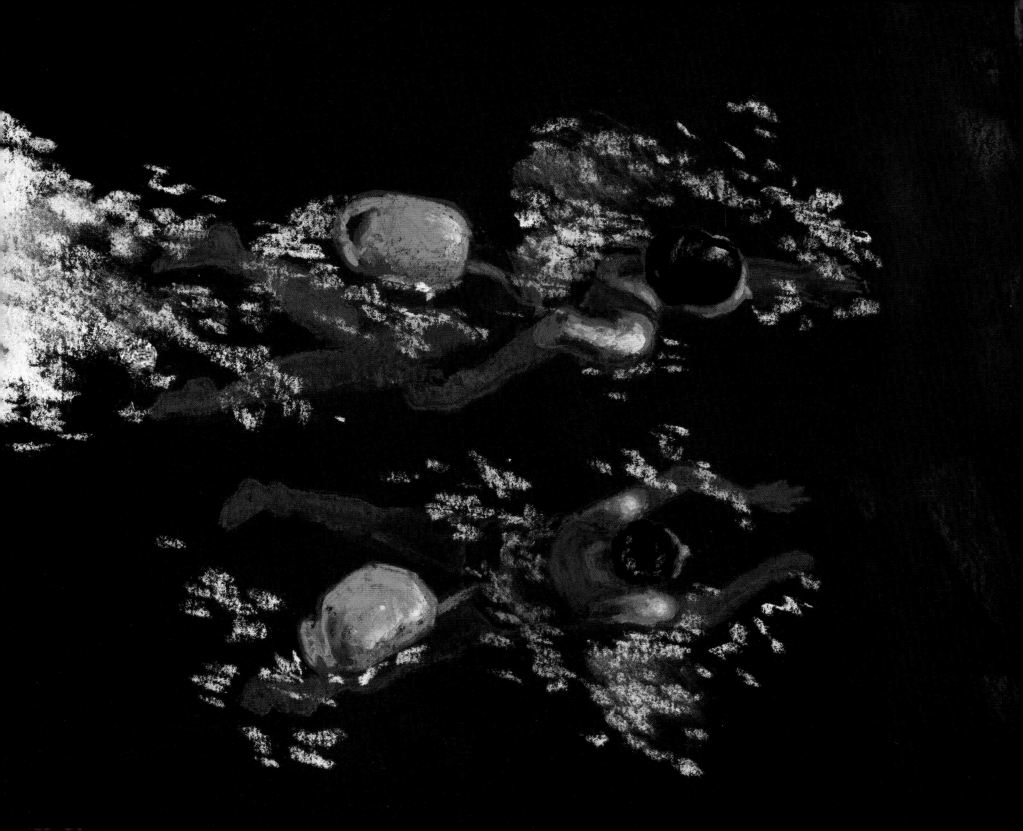

but

slipping,

bending,

listening,

reaching,

rising,

floating,

daring,

conquering,

we'll make it over.

When you can swim,
I'll take you there.

So swim, little one!

Me as a kid, trying to enjoy a trip to the local pool.

When I Learned to Swim

Growing up as an immigrant kid in Canada, there were reasons that the public pool never became a comfortable place for me. At the same time, swimming in nature never occurred to me as a possibility—it seemed unthinkable that anyone would go into water that cold!

Under the surface, my attitudes about swimming were a mishmash of layered and clashing cultural attitudes. As a child, I listened to stories my *Por-Por* (maternal grandmother) told about how she spent her childhood swimming in the rivers of Kalimantan, Indonesia—but also about how, later on, living in a China emerging from famine in the early 1960s, she forbade my mother from learning to swim at all for fear of the drownings and other accidental injuries and deaths common then among children. The aversion my mother developed toward swimming was what stuck with me, on top of my own anxieties: As a light-brown body among predominantly fair-skinned ones, I was so afraid of how my darker body features might look that I pretended to be sick to avoid school trips to the pool!

Three generations, three changing attitudes toward swimming. As I was creating this book, I kept thinking: *Is a book about swimming really just about swimming? Or is it also about our ideas of the world, and about the freedom for us to choose these ideas for ourselves?*

Much later, I came to love swimming when I took the plunge into rivers, ponds, lakes, and oceans. The cold, open water pushed me beyond my self-conscious feelings; fear was still there, but it found a place alongside my awe and wonder of nature's power. Quite the opposite of suggesting this is the only way to swim, I was struck by how my experience had depended upon location, access, and the encouragement of those around me.

I decided to make a book representing the freedom to discover swimming because representation is power: We can use it to depict the world we are striving for, before that world is a reality for everyone. By showing differently colored characters—as well as those representing different genders, ages, sizes, and abilities—all enjoying the pleasures of swimming in nature, I wished to say to anyone who has ever been made to feel that swimming is not for them: *Yes, this belongs to you, too.*

About the Illustrations

To create this book, I visited my favorite swimming holes and swam again and again. I am still not a very confident swimmer—it was especially scary to hold myself underwater to get good, long looks that would inspire my illustrations. To make sure I was safe, I first sought out information from local authorities on whether the water was free from hazards such as harmful algae or animals. Then, I went with a swimming buddy. I also wore a visibility buoy, which, along with life jackets for younger children, can be a useful aid, but not a substitute for respecting the water's natural forces.

The impressions of melding colors, beaming light, and swirling bubbles that I caught in my mind's eye were my best guides to drawing each scene. I also made sketches and took notes and photographs—and finally, I took care to leave each place as I found it, so I can observe it again. I invite you to do the same next time you're in nature: Do check out, but don't disturb, any other creature or plant life that may share the waters. Let your senses take it all in. Who knows—you might be onto a book of your own!

Enjoying a dip in a tannin-soaked lake, "researching" swirls, glittering light, and a golden tan.

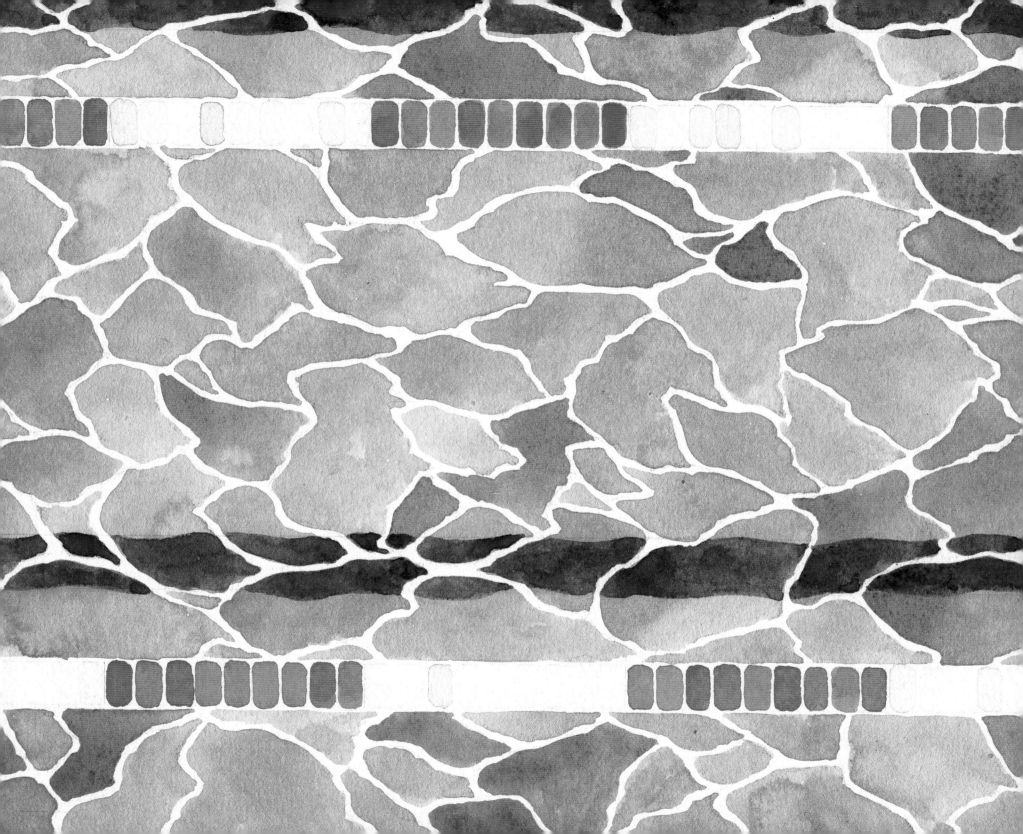